IVAN THE TERRIBLE

ANNE FINE

Illustrated by Philippe Dupasquier

EGMONT

You can visit Anne Fine's website
www.annefine.co.uk

and download free bookplates from
www.myhomelibrary.org

EGMONT

We bring stories to life

First published in Great Britain 2007
by Methuen Children's Books
This edition published 2018
by Egmont UK Limited
The Yellow Building, 1 Nicholas Road, London W11 4AN

Text copyright © Anne Fine 2007
Illustrations copyright © Philippe Dupasquier 2007

The moral rights of the author and illustrator have been asserted

ISBN 978 1 4052 8897 2

44906/13

A CIP catalogue record for this title is available from the British Library

Typeset by Avon DataSet Ltd, Bidford on Avon, Warwickshire
Printed and bound in Great Britain by the CPI Group

MIX
Paper from
responsible sources
FSC
www.fsc.org
FSC® C020471

For Boris

Contents

1

In which I meet Ivan and realise
I am in for a really hard time

The minute she spotted me, Mrs Blaizely's eyes lit up as if she were planning to eat me. 'Ah, Boris!'

I screeched to a halt in the corridor. 'Yes, Mrs Blaizely?'

'You speak Russian, don't you?'

'Yes,' I agreed. (No getting round that one with a mother called Galina Stepanova Rezotsky.)

'Right, then,' she told me. 'I think you're very probably the man for this job. Please come with me.'

I followed her into her office. It says **Mrs Elise Blaizely** on the door, and her name's put in every spelling test we have in our first year in school, till everyone gets it right.

There, waiting, was a boy my age. I'd seen him earlier at the school gates. His mother had been pointing at the sign that says **Welcome to St Edmund's** and he'd been trying to drag her away. You couldn't blame him. It's horrible starting at a new school halfway through term when everyone else knows everyone already. I'd had to do it myself, so when I saw him tugging at his mother's sleeve, I'd felt quite sorry for him.

Now he stood next to Mrs Blaizely, clutching what looked like a very stylish red leather-bound lunch box.

She pushed him forward gently.

'Boris,' she said. 'Meet Ivan. Ivan, meet Boris.'

'Hi,' I said.

'*Dobya dan*,' said Ivan.

'You see the problem?' Mrs Blaizely said. 'He speaks no English.'

I nodded (though I was thinking there probably wasn't a boy our age on the planet who hadn't seen enough adverts and films to make a stab at saying 'Hi').

'Just for a day or two . . .' said Mrs Blaizely in her coaxing tone.

I gave her one of my suspicious looks. 'Just for a day or two – *what*, exactly?' I asked as politely as I could.

'Chum him around,' said Mrs Blaizely. 'Explain to him all the things the teachers are saying. And then explain to the teachers what he says back.'

'Be his interpreter, you mean?'

She beamed at me. 'Yes. And, if he's

writing, you can translate for him. Just while we get him started. It will give him an idea of the sort of work you're doing in your classes. He'll soon get the hang of it.'

'But what about my own work?'

She didn't laugh. She's too polite. But she did raise an eyebrow because she knows that getting my own work done without being distracted hasn't always been top of my list of real worries.

And, as I say, I do remember exactly how awful it is to have to start off in a new class with twenty-five new people whose names you don't even know, especially if you can't speak a word of the language – not even 'Hi'.

'All right,' I said. 'I'll do it.'

'Good lad,' she praised me. Then, just as she was sending me back to my classroom, she thought of something else. 'Oh, by the way, Boris, please make sure the two of you are sitting in the front row during Assembly because I'll want to bring Ivan up on the stage to introduce him to everyone.'

'Righty-ho,' I said.

Mrs Blaizely's got a thing about running what she calls 'a civilized school'. She says she wants everyone at St Edmund's to have good manners and a positive attitude. So we began Assembly by singing that wimpy little song about remembering to be grateful for everything round us. (Lulu once wrote a joke version of it about *not* being grateful for empty beer cans, or sick on the pavements, or homework or dog poo. Mrs Shah said it was 'a brilliant spoof' and pinned it on the display board. She kept it up right through till Parents' Evening. Then she lost her nerve and suddenly it vanished.)

After we'd finished singing 'In Our Wonderful World', some of the children in the nursery put on a little show about being kind to animals and taking care of your pets. It wasn't up to much, but we all clapped to show our good manners and positive attitude. Then Mrs Blaizely begged us all to make less noise in the corridors and not drop so much litter. (We hear that so often it's practically our morning prayer.)

And then we came to our bit. Mrs Blaizely changed to her really bright and enthusiastic voice. 'I have someone to introduce to you,' she said to everyone. 'His name is Ivan and he comes from a huge country called Russia. Russia's so big that some snowy parts in the north are way up in the Arctic Circle while some parts in the south are so dry that they're desert.'

She beckoned to Ivan. 'Don't be shy. Come up here on stage so everyone can see you and know that they've got to be especially thoughtful and considerate until you've settled in.'

I gave Ivan a little push and he walked up the steps. I thought he'd just blush and stay at the side of the stage, shuffling his feet in an embarrassed fashion like everyone else who's ever been new to the school.

But no. He swept forward right to the middle, almost next to Mrs Blaizely, turned to face us all and did a sort of smart military bow from the waist.

Then he straightened up, threw his arms out wide, and said in the loudest, clearest Russian:

'Greetings to all you lowly shivering worms.'

I was still staring when Mrs Blaizely beckoned. She wanted me up the steps and standing next to Ivan. I didn't have

a choice.

'Now,' she said. 'Boris is going to tell us, in English, exactly what Ivan just said to us in Russian.'

She turned to me. 'Well, go on.'

I tell you frankly, this was my big mistake. If I'd just done it, just gone ahead and told her straight off: 'He said, "Greetings to all you lowly shivering worms",' I could have saved myself a heap of trouble.

But I couldn't do it. Look at it this way. There he was, on his first day in a new school. For all I knew, it could have been his very first week in a new country, his first day in his new house, almost his first words in his brand-new life (apart from arguing with his mother about whether or not to come through the school gates in the first place).

And he'd been called up to stand on

stage with everyone staring. I thought he must have panicked, and said something silly as a sort of joke, not realising that in our civilized school where everyone's supposed to have good manners and a positive attitude, it wasn't going to work, and everyone was going to end up staring at him even more.

Lowly shivering worms?

It's pretty *rude*. I couldn't let him get himself into everyone's bad books so quickly.

So I just told them: 'Ivan said, "Good morning, everyone".'

I thought we'd get away then. I thought Mrs Blaizely would nod at us, and we'd troop off the stage. I'd tick him off (in Russian) and we'd start the day again.

But no such luck, because Ivan hadn't finished. He stepped forward again.

'No doubt you'll all be half-witted

enough to welcome me amongst you,' he said (in Russian). 'Your tiny, dim-bulb brains are simply not capable of seeing that I have secret powers which I intend to use to turn the whole pack of you into my slaves.'

He beamed and gave another of his smart bows. There was a pause. Then Mrs Blaizely glanced at me enquiringly. 'Boris?'

I took a deep breath.

'I am delighted to be here,' I pretended to translate for Ivan. 'I think this school looks very nice. And everyone looks very kind and friendly. I really hope I'll settle in soon and make a whole load of new friends.'

'That's lovely,' said Mrs Blaizely. She turned to Ivan. 'And I'm sure everyone in this hall wants to join me in wishing you well and hoping you feel at home as soon as possible.'

Ivan turned to me. 'What did she say?'

I wasn't going to risk him coming out
with another barrage of insults. So I looked
Ivan in the eye and told him, 'She said,
"Watch your fat tongue, New Boy, or I'll
break off your arm and bash you with the
soggy end."'

I really hoped he'd look at Mrs Blaizely
with a new respect. But he just grinned and
walked down the steps from the stage.

Feeling a bit of a wally, I followed him.

End of Assembly. And thank heaven for that.

2

In which I decide I am a hot dinner and Ivan must be a packed lunch

We walked back to the classroom in single file. (I think Mr Hardy must have been raised in the army: he keeps forgetting we're 'a civilized school' and makes us do everything in lines.)

I told him I'd been given the job of being Ivan's interpreter all day, and he looked horrified. 'Does that mean you two will have to sit together?'

I shrugged. I wasn't keen on the idea myself, but didn't see how else the job could be done.

Mr Hardy scowled. He'd obviously forgotten to have 'a positive attitude' as well. 'You realise that means I'm going to have to move everyone round.'

Honestly! The fuss he made, you would have thought I'd said we had to do our written work underwater. He practically turned all the desk changing into a military exercise, barking out orders. (He'd forgotten the 'good manners' bit, too.) But finally he'd put Ivan in my old place, he'd moved me into Oriole's seat, and he'd bumped everyone else one chair along, right to the end of the row.

Ivan was flapping about a bit, but only till he had found a safe enough place for his precious red leather-bound lunch box.

Then we were settled.

'Right,' Mr Hardy said. 'Now stand up, Ivan, and tell us your full name slowly and carefully so we can learn exactly how to say it so it sounds right to you.'

I started telling Ivan what he was supposed to do.

'No need to chatter,' Mr Hardy said.

'I wasn't chattering,' I protested. 'I was *interpreting*. I was just letting him know what you *said*.'

'Oh, sorry,' said Mr Hardy. 'I forgot we needed that bit. I suppose you'd better stand up, too.'

'No, really,' I assured him. 'There's no need.'

'Stand up, please, Boris,' Mr Hardy said.

So then there were the two of us, standing together in a sea of curious faces.

'Well, go on,' said Mr Hardy, forgetting the good manners bit again. 'Get on with it. Much as I'd like to gaze upon your two beauteous countenances all morning, we do have work to do.'

I turned to Ivan and told him (in Russian): 'Tell everyone your whole name and do it slowly and clearly, so they can hear it properly.'

Ivan smiled warmly round at everyone. Most of them smiled back. They all knew everyone feels a little embarrassed when they have to say their name aloud to strangers. Then Ivan took a deep breath and declared (in Russian): 'I am Count Ivan Alexander Nicoleyavitch Polinitstzyn, Master of Thrones, Slayer of Enemies, Commander of Armies, Lord of the Wise, Fountain of –'

'Just your full name will do,' I

interrupted him.

He completely ignored me.

'Fountain of National Pride. And be warned, you weak-witted maggots. For I have come to trample you and your grandmothers under my heel. I come to kill your pets and bite off your right hands. I come to strew deadly bacteria over your foodstuffs and steal your cousins' babies. I come –'

'What *is* he saying?' Mr Hardy demanded. 'Nobody's name can be *that* long.'

This is my chance, I thought. And then, almost at once, I realised that it wasn't. Ivan had smiled round at everyone so warmly before he began that no one would ever believe me if I said that he'd been threatening to bite off their right hands.

But I could at least show Ivan

Alexander Nicoleyavitch Polinitstzyn how annoying it is when people don't say what they're supposed to say.

'His name is Ivan Alex Nick Polly,' I simplified out of spite. 'And all the rest of it was just a heap of stuff about how to pronounce it.'

'Well, you can tell young Ivan here,' said Mr Hardy, 'that I can say Ivan Alex Nick Polly perfectly well already.' He turned to Lulu. 'And so can you, Lulu, can't you?'

'Yes,' Lulu said. 'No problem there. Ivan Alex Nick Polly. See? I just did it!'

Ivan gave Lulu one of his smart little bows from the waist, along with a radiant smile. 'You will die first,' he warned her.

'He says, "Jolly good,"' I said.

'Yusef?' asked Mr Hardy. 'Can you say it too?'

'Ivan Alex Nick Polly,' said Yusef.

Ivan turned his way, still beaming. 'And you will die next.'

'He says that sounds fine,' I told Yusef.

Then Ivan and I both sat down. I was *exhausted*. I'd saved him in Assembly because I thought he might be nervous or angry, or in a state because of coming here. I had felt *sorry* for him. Now I felt sorry for *me*. I'd missed at least three good chances to sneak on him and by now I'd somehow made him sound so amiable and nice and polite that if I changed tack and started on about him saying he had come to slay our cousins' babies and kill our pets and trample on our grandmothers, no one was ever going to believe me.

They'd think I was making it up because I was bored with interpreting, and wanted to get back to spending time with my own friends.

No. I was stuck.

Unless he changed his ways . . .

Mrs Blaizely wants this to be a civilized school, so I decided to try and persuade him in a civilized fashion.

'Listen,' I said (in Russian). 'This isn't easy for me.'

He turned. 'What isn't easy?'

'Telling them what you're saying.'

He stared. 'Why? You speak Russian. And you speak English. What is the problem?'

'It's not the *interpreting*,' I told him. 'It's the words you *say*. All that stuff about putting deadly bacteria on their food and –'

'Strewing,' he corrected me. '"To put" is merely to place something somewhere. There is a whole lot more to strewing.' He made an expansive gesture to show me. 'It is more like spreading corn.'

'All *right*,' I said irritably. '*Strewing*.

And biting off right hands. And –'

Mr Hardy appeared at my shoulder.

'Have you two finished gassing? Because, if you have, perhaps the rest of us can get on with things.'

He went back to the front and turned to the whole class.

'Now I've counted up the lunch numbers, but there's something fishy about the figures so I want to go through it again.

Stand up if you're a hot dinner.'

I was one of the ones who stood up.

Ivan gazed at me enquiringly.

'I'm a hot dinner,' I explained (in Russian).

Ivan looked mystifed. 'I beg your pardon?'

I tried to explain. 'You see, Mr Hardy wants to count all over again. So everyone standing up is a hot dinner.'

'Ah, I see,' Ivan told me bitterly. 'You try to forbid me to claim to be Master of Thrones, Lord of the Wise or Fountain of National Pride. But you and all your classmates here can claim to be –' His lip curled horribly as he spat out the words. 'Hot dinners!'

Put like that, it did sound a little daft, so I sat down.

'Boris!' roared Mr Hardy. 'I am trying to *count*. Stop bobbing up and down. Are you a hot dinner, or aren't you? And what about your friend?'

The way I saw it, this was my big chance for ten minutes rest at lunch time. After all, Ivan had his precious red leather-bound lunch box. And all the people who have hot dinners sit at a separate table.

So I made the choice.

'I'm a hot dinner,' I told Mr Hardy firmly. 'And Ivan here is a packed lunch.'

3

In which I sing songs to toddlers
about death, violence, poverty, hunger,
beatings and cruelty to animals

We did maths first. Miss Honeyman
handed round our workbooks and found
one for Ivan as well. 'I know we haven't
had time to find out what he knows and
what he doesn't,' she said to me. 'But tell
him to make a start on this before he goes
over to the annexe for his assessment.'

I turned to Ivan and explained.

'Go over to where?' he asked.

I pointed out of the window. 'See that
building there? It's called the annexe. The
nursery children are all at one end, and the
assessment room is at the other.'

'Oh, right,' he said. Shrugging, he
opened his workbook and started working

through it. (That is exactly what he did. He began on page one, glanced at each sum for a moment, wrote down the answers one by one, then turned each page.)

I watched in fascination.

'You're very good with numbers,' I told him (in Russian).

He put his finger down to mark his place and raised his head. 'Did you suppose that we're still using bacon for bank notes?'

'No,' I assured him. 'I'm just amazed at how fast you can do them.'

'Perhaps I've got them all wrong!' he

told me. (But you could tell from the way he said it that it was some sort of Russian 'joke'.)

I raised my hand. 'Miss Honeyman! Miss Honeyman! Ivan has already finished the workbook you gave him.'

Miss Honeyman strolled over, picked up Ivan's book and inspected his answers.

'Tell him he's finding this workbook too easy,' she told me.

When I told him, he shrugged. 'Tell her another way to look at it is that the book is written for shallow-brained fools.'

I thought she might think I'd made that bit up, and so I skipped it and simply told Miss Honeyman that Ivan thought so too.

Miss Honeyman sighed. 'The sooner we find out exactly where he is in everything, the better. Boris, as soon as the bell rings I want you to take Ivan over to the annexe. I'll get my next class settled and join you as soon as I can.'

She brought Ivan another workbook to pass the time till the bell rang. He started ploughing through that, though it had things in it I'd never seen.

'That looks pretty difficult,' I said to him.

He raised an eyebrow. 'Do you and the rest of the class take special pills each day, to stay so stupid?'

'No,' I snapped. (I was beginning to find it rather hard to stick to good manners.)

'Then perhaps it's something in the water.'

I couldn't work out if he was being serious, or being rude. So, rather than be uncivilized and thump him really hard on his first day, I went back to my workbook and kept at it until the bell rang.

'Right,' I reminded him. 'Now we have

to go off to the annexe.'

Ivan scrabbled under his desk for his red leather-bound lunch box.

'You won't need that,' I told him. 'We're not staying all day.'

Rather reluctantly, he put it down and followed me. I didn't waste any more time. I *love* going to the annexe because, from our side of the school, you can only get to it by walking through the nursery. The minute you open the door, there's the fat warm smell of modelling clay and poster paints, and all the little ones drop whatever it is that they're doing to swarm around you. I love their chubby pink faces and the sweet way some of them take an age even to get started on what they want to say. I love the way they paw you, and lean against you as if you were their very own brother, and carry huge picture books up to you and shove them in your lap and give you orders

– 'Now read this to me!' – as if they were all royal princelings, and you were just some sort of slave.

We went through the swing doors that you can only open if you are tall enough to reach the latch.

'Ivan has come to be assessed,' I told Mrs Nash. 'We have to wait for Miss Honeyman.'

Already the little ones were flocking like seagulls gathering round two huge

crusts.

'Righty-ho,' said Mrs Nash. 'Well, till she comes, you might as well do something useful.' She handed me *The Great Big Book of Nursery Rhymes*. 'Here, Boris. While I'm setting things up for the ones who'll be starting with finger paints, you start a little sing-song with everyone who's left over.'

The little ones kept swarming.

'They can't *all* be left over,' I argued, panicking a little. But Mrs Nash had

already turned away, so I made them sit on the rug. I dragged two fat yellow beanbags over for me and Ivan. I opened up the book.

'We'll start with *Three Blind Mice*,' I told them.

Off we went:

Three blind mice, three blind mice,
See how they run, see how they run.
They all ran after the farmer's wife
Who cut off their tails with a carving
knife —

The minute we got to that bit, Ivan shifted his beanbag so he could see the pictures better. Then he dug in his pocket and drew out a tiny dictionary with 'Russian into English, English into Russian' printed on the cover.

I saw him glance again at the picture of the three blind mice running off without their tails. He flicked through the dictionary, ran his finger down a page, then mouthed the word he was interested in silently to himself as the little ones and I warbled to the end of the nursery rhyme.

Did you ever see such a thing in your life
As three blind mice?

I turned the page. Next came *Tom, Tom, the Piper's Son*. Ivan leaned forward to inspect the picture, then said to me (in Russian), 'I could see from the picture that the last song was about cruelty to animals. Tell me about this one.'

I felt obliged to explain the words of

Tom, Tom, the Piper's Son, and then the little ones and I sang it together.

Tom, Tom, the piper's son
Stole a pig and away he ran.
The pig was eat, and Tom
was beat
And Tom went crying
down the street.

'Very nice,' Ivan said to me. 'Theft. Child beating. Very suitable for little children.'

Again, he thumbed through his pocket dictionary while the nursery children and I moved on to *Humpty Dumpty.*

'Please sing it again,' Ivan begged us. He was staring, baffled, first at the picture of the smartly dressed egg sitting on a wall, then at the page which showed Humpty Dumpty smashed to pieces after his great fall, while all the king's horses and all the king's men stood round looking worried and helpless.

It didn't seem good manners to refuse, so I had to tell the little ones, 'He'd like to hear that one a second time.'

Happily they started up again.

Humpty Dumpty
sat on a wall.
Humpty Dumpty had a
great fall
All the king's horses and
all the king's men
Couldn't put Humpty
together again.

The next nursery rhyme we sang was *Sing a Song of Sixpence*. I felt quite confident through all the bits about the king in

his counting house counting up his money and the queen in her parlour eating bread and honey. It sounded a whole lot more civilized. But as soon as we reached the last verse I realised we were in trouble, and, sure enough, the little ones were soon chanting the last two lines:

The maid was in the garden hanging
out the clothes,
When down came a
blackbird and pecked
off her nose.

Ivan was flicking through his dictionary again. '*Aha*!' I heard him mutter to himself. 'A song about wrecked beauty. More senseless waste and damage, like the cruelly sliced-off mouse tails and the poor egg man crushed beyond repair.'

He shook his head in sorrow, like someone who'd found himself among a tribe of savages who knew no better.

Hastily I turned over to the next page. But it was *Peter, Peter, Pumpkin Eater*. I rushed to turn over again, but all the little ones had already begun to sing:

> *Peter, Peter, Pumpkin Eater,*
> *Had a wife and couldn't keep her.*
> *He put her in a pumpkin shell*
> *And there he kept her very well.*

'I see,' mused Ivan, who had been peering closely at the illustration as they were singing. 'This greedy Peter man is so vile in nature that his wife wants to leave him, so he locks her up instead . . .'

Pretending I hadn't heard, I turned the page.

Oh, great choice! *Solomon Grundy*.

None of the little ones knew it, so I had to sing it all by myself.

Solomon Grundy,
Born on a Monday,
Christened on Tuesday,
Married on Wednesday,
Took ill on Thursday,
Worse on Friday,
Died on Saturday,
Buried on Sunday:
That was the end
Of Solomon Grundy.

'Translate it, please,' said Ivan.

I didn't feel I had a choice, so I

translated it while all the little ones rolled on the mat, getting bored.

'Ah,' Ivan said. 'I see the point. This song says that even in the cradle one is not too young to be told that life is nothing more than a dreary journey towards a grim and hollow end.'

Opening the tiny dictionary, he looked up one or two more words while absent-mindedly humming a snatch from *Sing a Song of Sixpence*.

I was quite glad to see Miss Honeyman come through the door.

It felt like *rescue*.

4

In which I as good as threaten Ivan with poisonous pizza

Ivan's assessment went on for *ever*. Some of the tests he could do by himself, so long as I explained at the start what he was supposed to be doing. At other times we had to go through the questions one by one, with me telling Miss Honeyman his answers.

We worked all through break-time ('You don't mind, do you, Boris?') and the only good moment was when Mrs Nash brought Miss Honeyman a cup of coffee on a tray with lots of biscuits, and Ivan and I got the biscuits.

Finally we reached the end and Miss Honeyman gathered up the papers. 'They won't take long to sort out,' she told me as we walked back through the nursery. 'Tell Ivan that by the end of the day, Mrs Blaizely will know what's best for him.'

She hurried off. We followed her out of the annexe and I passed the message on to Ivan.

'Best for me,' I heard him muttering, 'would be a mother who will listen when her son points out her stupid mistake.'

I was about to ask him what he meant when he pointed over the fence to the big bouncy castle the janitor had set up ready for our Autumn Fair.

'What's that?' asked Ivan.

I don't know what came over me except that I was hungry and I'd had enough of Ivan and his opinions. He thought our workbooks were for fools, our nursery rhymes were weirdly stuffed with violence and cruelty, and his mother was too stupid to listen to a word he said. It seemed to me that Ivan was just so full of himself that it would almost be *civilized* to bring him down a peg or two.

So I looked at the bouncy castle. 'It's a rock sculpture,' I told him. 'It weighs twenty-seven tons. It took a crane to bring it in and fifteen strong men just to swing it round on its chains to make it face the right way before they lowered it onto the ground.'

'Is that so?' said Ivan. (I couldn't tell from the look on his face if he was scoffing or a little bit impressed.)

We walked past the hall. The playground side is like a wall of glass, so you can see what's going on inside.

'We do gymnastics in there,' I said to

Ivan. 'For the first two classes of every term, we're allowed to wear shorts and a T-shirt. But after that we have to do the lessons stark naked.'

'Really?'

'Really,' I said.

We strolled past the kitchens. Mr and Mrs Fuller waved at me through the window. (When I'm not a packed lunch, I'm one of their best customers. I have been known to have *thirds*.)

'See them?' I whispered to Ivan. (Oh, I was really taking revenge on him now.) 'They're not just looking happy because they're nice people. Oh no. They're pleased because they've just got out of jail after poisoning her mother to get their hands on her money. Now here they are back again, cooking our dinners.'

Mr Fuller leaned out of the window. 'Pizza today, Boris!'

I gave him the thumbs up. 'Save me a big slice!' Then I turned to Ivan. 'You must know *some* English words. You must at least know the word "pizza".'

Ivan looked down his nose at me. 'The word "pizza" is Italian.'

I was *exasperated*. It seemed to me that if he didn't make a stab at speaking English soon, I could be walking round with him for weeks and weeks. But now we were almost across the playground and back in the school so, reminded of Mrs Blaizely, I tried to take a positive attitude. 'Well, what about those words you were looking up while I was singing all those nursery rhymes? You must know those.'

'Ah, yes,' said Ivan. 'During your little sing-song, I looked up quite a lot of useful little words.' He tried them out carefully in

English. '"Crush". "Bludgeon". "Flail".
And, of course, "mutilate".'

I was a bit surprised. They didn't sound
the sort of words you'd pick up from a
nursery sing-song.

'"Crush?"'

'The poor egg man in the bow tie.
Crushed beyond repair.'

'"Bludgeon?"'

'The man who owned the pig. He had
a big stick and I think it would be fair to say
that he was bludgeoning the young boy
Tom. Very hard.'

'What about "mutilate?"'

He looked surprised I'd even asked.
'Well, what would *you* call slicing off mice
tails and pecking off maids' noses?'

I didn't ask about 'flail'. I've lived in
Britain since my second birthday, and even
I don't really know what 'flail' means. I just
said sourly, 'Oh, very useful! Learning

"crush" and "flail" and "mutilate".'

'The stupid pills are clearly working well today,' crowed Ivan. 'You have forgotten "bludgeon".'

I knew if it came to a 'being nasty' battle, he'd win hands down. So I went back to being positive. 'Ivan, I just think that, if you're going to have to live here, it would be far more useful to learn a few more *basic* words.'

'Like what?'

I shrugged. '*I* don't know. Things like –' I had a quick think. 'Things like –' I said them in English,

'"teapot" and "sheep" and "boy" and "thumb".'

He looked at me blankly and asked, 'What is this "teapot" and "sheep" and "boy" and "thumb"?'

I spent a moment translating each of them in turn. Then, carefully he repeated them after me in English. '"Teapot". "Sheep". "Boy". "Thumb".'

'That's it!' I said, proud that my being positive had worked so well. 'You've got them!'

'Excellent!' he said. 'Then I will add them now to my collection.'

We walked through the swing doors into the main school corridor. Beside me, almost thoughtfully, Ivan was muttering.

'I *crush* the teapot. I *flail* the sheep. I *bludgeon* the boy. I *mutilate* the thumb.'

I walked a little faster. (Actually, I almost *ran*.)

5

In which I remember a little about Vladivostock and learn a lot about litter

By the time we got back into class, the rest had their heads down, working. Miss Honeyman had written the title 'Something Very Close To Me' up on the board, and told everybody they had to cover at least two sides of paper before the bell rang.

She didn't worry about me. (She knows how fast I can write.) But she did shoot a worried look at Ivan.

'Tell him that, just this once, he can write it in Russian,' she told me. 'Just till we know the results of his assessment.'

So I told Ivan what we had to do.

Ivan looked thoughtful. '"Something

Very Close To Me"?'

'Yes,' I said. 'You could pick anything. Your home town. Your football team. Your pet gerbil.'

'Something very close to me . . .'

He stared around him for a bit, and then got going. The next half hour was quite restful really. I wrote about my baby sister, Natasha. Mum puts her in my bed whenever she can't sleep. Natasha twirls my hair in her fingers. And stabs me with her elbows. *And* she snores. *And* works her way over to my side. *And* hiccups. So there was quite a lot to complain about, and by the time Miss Honeyman asked us to 'Start to round it off now, please', I was most of the way down my second sheet of paper.

Ivan was on his third.

'You have to stop now,' I warned him.

He came to a halt with a flourish, then laid down his pen and sat back in his chair.

Miss Honeyman chose Arthur to read his piece of work out first. It was about his cat, Brandy. Then Lulu read out hers. It was about the wheelchair that she's been stuck in since she was four. Then I read mine. Miss Honeyman told me, 'That's very full of feeling, Boris!'

And then she had the bright idea of getting me to read out Ivan's.

'Don't bother with the Russian,' she told me. 'Just translate it so we'll all know a little bit more about what's close to Ivan.'

I reached for his paper. Under the Russian for 'Something Very Close To Me', he'd written:

'What is close to me is all the disgusting little splodges of dried-up, chewed gum that Boris stuck under this desk during the weeks he was sitting here.'

I gave him a look. He was *definitely* smirking. I didn't see why I should let him

get me into trouble for chewing gum in class without putting up a bit of a fight. But I decided there was a very civilized way to save myself, using good manners and a positive attitude.

'Right,' I told everyone. 'Ivan has written: "What's closest to me is Vladivostock, the great port city in the far east of Russia, where I was born."'

He could have been born in a barrel floating down the Volga for all I knew. But my mum came from Vladivostock. I might not be totally up to date on the place, but after spending hours on her knee hearing old stories about her childhood, I could at least have a go.

Miss Honeyman had turned to look at Ivan fondly. 'That's very sweet and loyal of him,' she said, 'to choose his own country to write about.'

Ivan gave her a beaming smile back.

'Go on,' said Miss Honeyman. 'Read out the next bit, Boris.'

The next bit said, '*I find these grey lumps of chewed matter, with Boris's teethmarks still in them, even more offensive than the sweet wrappers and pencil sharpenings that he has so unthinkingly strewn around all four legs of what is now my chair.*'

I definitely wasn't going to read out that. So what I said was: '"Vladivostock is noted for its huge harbour, which freezes up for three months every year, and for its vast and useful railway station. There is also an excellent museum."'

The class were beginning to yawn now. Even Miss Honeyman's eyes were glazing over.

'Fascinating,' she murmured.

I glanced through the next chunk of Ivan's Russian.

'Clearly the school takes a very casual attitude towards cleanliness. I notice that, although it has not rained today, the floor tiles are thick with muddy footprints. It leads me to wonder if British parents have failed to explain to their children the concept of wiping their feet.'

'"Vladivostock",' I pretended to read out, '"has a thriving theatre. There are plenty of cinemas and of course, in

the thick of winter, there will be sledding, and skating along the great river –'"

I couldn't remember the name of Vladivostock's river, so I just finished up, 'along the great river Fred.'

Miss Honeyman looked startled. 'The great river *Fred*?'

'That's what he's written,' I told her, beaming in my turn. And it was a real smile. I felt quite positive about protecting Ivan this time because I was doing it only to protect myself.

'Perhaps the river was named after one of their great old Russian Czars,' said Miss Honeyman. 'Like Alexander the Blessed. Or Ivan the Terrible. Or Peter the Great.'

'I expect it was,' I said. 'Perhaps after Fred the Almost-Forgotten.'

'Well,' Miss Honeyman said hopefully. 'Have we nearly come to the end of Ivan's piece of writing?'

I glanced down. There was a paragraph or two about my grubby woollen jumper, my unwashed hands and bitten fingernails, and all the stains on the desk. There was a sentence or two about the lack of ventilation generally, and a plea for some form of air freshener to be introduced to make things nicer.

'There's not much more,' I said. 'Just one last sentence about the excellent sewerage system, and how the Chamber of

Commerce in Vladivostock does its very best to promote the image of the city abroad.'

'That's lovely, dear,' said Miss Honeyman faintly.

I think I'd beaten her into the ground because, rather than risk worse, she started collecting all the sheets, lined us up by the door, and sent us off early to pick up some litter before lunch break.

6

In which Ivan chats to the
teachers over an excellent lunch, and I
choke to death on cold pizza

Because of the litter, we were the last class
to reach the dining hall. 'You go and sit
over there,' I said to Ivan. 'And I queue for
my food here.'

'I'm hungry too,' said Ivan.

I pointed to the lunch box he was
clutching. 'You eat whatever you've got in
there.'

Ivan flipped back the catches. Inside
the red leather-bound box lay a few black
shiny tubes on a bed of black velvet. Some
of them looked as if they screwed together
and most had shining silver finger plates
down one side or the other.

'That's not a packed lunch,' I said.

'No. It's an oboe.'

'Well, you can't eat that.' I sighed. 'Come on, then. I suppose you'd better just turn into a hot dinner and hope there's enough to go round.'

We joined the queue. While we were standing in line, Bob Foster sidled past, on his way out. There was a blob of spaghetti sauce on his shirt, a dribble of yoghurt down his sleeve, and sprinkles of bread on his jumper.

'Oh, look!' said Ivan. 'What a good idea! A walking menu!'

I ignored the sarcasm and turned back to the counter. Now we were close enough to the front of the queue to see the big square dishes that hold the hot meals. Apart from the pizza Mr Fuller had promised me, there were small balls of pasta in tomato sauce, or sausages and mashed potato.

Mrs Fuller asked Ivan, 'What would

you like?'

'You have to choose one,' I told him.

'I'll have the eyeballs swimming in their own blood,' said Ivan.

'He'll have the pasta in tomato sauce,' I said.

Mrs Fuller scooped a generous helping onto Ivan's plate. 'Do you fancy any of the salads?'

'A small serving of grass clippings, please.'

'A bit of the chopped lettuce,' I translated.

'And one of your small grey stones.'

'And a freshly baked roll, please.'

'Jolly good!' she said, and beamed at Ivan.

'I'll have pizza and salad, please,' I told her.

She glanced down at the one manky dried-up slice left in the pan. 'Hang on a minute, Boris. I know how much you love pizza. I'll just get a fresh tray.'

She turned her back to slide the next tray off the serving hatch.

'What is she doing?' asked Ivan. 'Should we be watching her very closely indeed, in case she's sprinkling on poison?'

Mrs Fuller turned back to me. 'What did he say?'

I didn't want to lose my lovely big fat

slice of pizza still hot from the oven just because Mrs Fuller was offended. And it was only because of my joke about her poisoning her mother that Ivan was suspicious anyway. So I just told her, 'Ivan said it looked delicious and, next time you serve pizza, that's what he's going to have.' I turned to him. 'Don't bother waiting for me. Just take your tray, and see if you can find a table with two empty spaces.'

'Right you are,' he said. And by the time I'd heaped enough salad and tomatoes onto my plate, he'd vanished.

I stood with my pizza getting cold, scanning the busy dining hall to try to find him.

Finally I noticed him. He'd only chosen to take a seat at the teachers' table! They were all sitting there, not quite sure what to do, and trying to pretend it wasn't anything special. It was his first day, after all. And how can you tactfully tick off a boy who doesn't understand a word you say?

Not only that, but (so far as I know) there isn't any actual *rule* that says we can't sit with the teachers.

We just *don't*.

I didn't know what to do, so in the end I just went over and hovered behind him with my tray.

Mr Hardy sighed. 'Well, sit down, Boris. Since Ivan's already halfway through his meal, you might as well join us, too.'

I wasn't going to argue because my lovely pizza was getting cold. I pulled up a chair and dived in. I cut off a square of pizza and stabbed it with my fork. Ivan was watching me closely, but I didn't realise why till the very last moment.

Just as I raised the fork towards my mouth, he stretched out a hand and laid it on my arm to stop me. Gazing earnestly into my eyes, he said in urgent tones: 'Please tell the teachers that, in my opinion, this is excellent food. It tastes so nice. And it is splendidly public-spirited of the school

staff to make themselves, and all the young people in their care, so very vulnerable by giving two convicted murderers their jobs back, even after they've already left one sickening trail of death behind them.'

I knew he was only saying it to stop me eating. But he had managed to make his message sound so very important that the teachers were staring expectantly, waiting for me to translate it.

I looked down at my pizza. I could practically *watch* it curling at the edges and congealing on top.

'He says he really likes the grub,' I muttered briefly.

'Are you sure you're interpreting properly?' Mr Hardy asked me suspiciously. 'I thought that what he said sounded a whole lot longer than, "I like the grub".'

Sighing, I put down my fork. Be

positive, I told myself. There will be other chances to eat pizza while it's still hot, so be polite; be civilized. Of course I couldn't translate Ivan's speech exactly – that would have got me into hot water because of the joke about poison. I looked at Ivan, who was grinning broadly as if he reckoned this time he had well and truly stumped me.

I wasn't going to let him think he had one over on me. So I thought fast. 'He said that his dear, dead grandmother often used to make tomato sauce in her little thatched cottage in the forest. She always put a few more herbs in it than this sauce seems to have. But, he says, if he is honest (and with no disrespect at all to his late grandmother) he rather thinks he might prefer it this way. And perhaps, now he comes to consider, his grandmother's recipe was a little *too* aromatic – even though, in his opinion, she was generally a very fine cook indeed.'

That bored them rigid. They tried to be good-mannered and civilized, but really they couldn't turn away fast enough to talk among themselves.

I finally went back to eating my stone-cold pizza. But the danger wasn't over. Just as Ivan was clearing the last of the sauce off his plate with the crust of his roll, he leaned over the table and asked Mr Hardy conversationally, 'Are you planning on eating that yoghurt? Because, if not, I wouldn't mind having it myself.'

I choked on my pizza. Mr Hardy raised an eyebrow in my direction. I thought at first he might be worrying about the fact that I was clearly dying of asphyxiation. But no. He simply wanted to know what Ivan had said.

I cleared my throat. At least that gave me time to think. And I did realise I'd completely forgotten to tell Ivan about the yoghurts. If he didn't manage to get Mr Hardy's, I'd have to be good-mannered enough to offer to share mine.

I took the positive approach. Tactful. 'Ivan just said he hadn't realised there was such a thing as bilberry yoghurt. He was just wondering what it tastes like.'

Sighing, Mr Hardy pushed it over.

'Thank you,' said Ivan. 'Thank you very much.'

'Thank you,' I said in English. 'Thank you very much.'

I stared at Ivan. Ivan stared at me. I think we were both astonished. He was so pleased to get the yoghurt he had forgotten to say something rude. And I had realised that, for the first time ever, I'd actually translated what he'd said.

The very first time ever!

7

In which we all sing one song and Ivan sings another

After lunch, it was singing – my favourite lesson of the week. I don't care who I stand beside or what we sing. It all makes me feel happy.

First Mr Hardy arranged us into lines, then he gave out the music books.

The first song was 'What a Happy Day It Is'. We bashed it out. Those of us who adore singing made double the noise to make up for the one or two who can't be bothered and simply mouth the words.

When we got to the end, Ivan nudged me.

'That song,' he whispered (in Russian). 'It just thumps on and on. Was it composed especially to be sung by the tone-deaf?'

'What's bothering Ivan?' Mr Hardy asked.

I didn't want Mr Hardy to waste a single moment of my favourite lesson giving Ivan a lecture about being polite and taking a positive attitude.

So I said, 'Oh, he just wants to know what the words mean.'

'Well, tell him!' said Mr Hardy. 'Then we can sing it for him again.'

So I translated the first verse:

> "*Oh, what a happy day it is!*
> *Happy day,*
> *Happy day.*
> *Oh, what a happy day it is.*
> *I'm glad to be alive-oh!*""

Ivan was staring at me, so I translated the second verse:

"'Oh, what a lucky child am I!
Lucky child,
Lucky child.
Oh, what a lucky child am I.
I'm glad to be alive-oh!'"

'Stop!' Ivan begged me. 'Stop! I see the words were written particularly to be sung by idiots. I'll try to pick it up as we go along.'

'He's all right now,' I said to Mr Hardy. 'In fact, he would quite like us to get back to singing.'

'Right, then,' said Mr Hardy. 'All together now! Big voices, please!'

And off we went again. I found it a bit unnerving, because although coming in one ear I could hear all that stuff about having a happy day and being a lucky child, there was something quite loud in Russian coming in the other:

"'Oh, I will lop off all your heads,
All your heads,
All your heads,
Oh, I will lop off all your heads!
I'm proud to be a ty-rant!

And I will build a
heap of skulls,
Heap of skulls,
Heap of skulls.
Yes, I will build a
heap of skulls
And plant my
flag on top-oh!'"

Mr Hardy was
delighted. 'Tell
him he made an
excellent stab of joining in there,
and he has a really nice singing voice.'

The last thing I felt like doing was passing on a compliment to the very person who'd spoiled the song for me. So I told Ivan, 'He says you sing like a corncrake, and if you do that again you will find his yellow fangs locked in your throat.'

'I think you're lying,' Ivan said.

'I think you're a pain,' I retorted.

'When you two good mates have stopped having your friendly little chat,' said Mr Hardy, 'we'll go on to the next song.'

Just as he sounded the first note on the

piano, the door behind us swung open. Everyone turned to gawp.

It was Mrs Blaizely. In her hand was one of the seven separate assessment sheets Ivan had done in the annexe. 'Can I borrow Boris for a moment, Mr Hardy? I hope you don't mind.'

'Not at all,' said Mr Hardy expansively. 'Feel free to keep him as long as you like.'

I stepped out of line. Out of sheer habit, Ivan stepped out of line to join me.

Mrs Blaizely gave him a worried look, then said, 'Well, actually, I might need Ivan too. So I suppose he'd better come as well.'

'That's a real shame,' said Mr Hardy. 'He was a welcome addition to the choir. We were about to start on "See the Bright Butterfly!" and I think he'd have liked that.'

I was so cross that, as we were going out of the door, I nearly said to Ivan, 'Mr

Hardy said he's glad to be rid of you before we all get on to singing our very favourite: "Road of Blood and Gore."'

But Mrs Blaizely had turned her worried look on me and added kindly, 'I know how much you love your singing lessons, Boris. And so I promise you this won't take long. It's only one small question.'

So I was civilized and I just sighed.

8

In which Ivan sits with his back to
us and writes busily at the table

We went with Mrs Blaizely to her office.
Even before we were inside, her phone was
ringing. Mrs Blaizely hurried to her desk to
take the call while Ivan and I stood waiting.
On the table beside us were piles of cards
with 'St Edmund's School – Term Report'
printed across the top. The boxes that said
'Pupil's Name' had been filled in already,
but nothing else.

Ivan picked up a couple of the cards.
'So what are these?'

'Those are report cards,' I told him.

'Reporting on
what?' he asked. 'On
quality of work? Or
on behaviour?'

'Pretty well everything.' I translated the words in the column that ran down one side: Reading, Writing, Sports, General Attitude – that sort of thing. Then I translated the words that ran in order across the grid at the top: Excellent, Very Good, Good, Satisfactory, More Effort Needed – and the one the teachers don't tick very often because they're trying to be positive: Unsatisfactory.

He pointed to the blank box printed underneath. 'And what is this?'

'That's just a space. For comments.'

'What sort of comments?'

'You know,' I said. 'The exact same thing you must have had in your old school. Telling you off in a civilized and good-mannered way. "It will help Katarina and everyone else in the school when she finally learns not to run in the corridors." "Tanya would find the work a lot easier if she paid more attention in class." That sort of thing.'

'I see.'

Mrs Blaizely broke off from her call. 'Don't waste your time, boys. Boris, why don't you teach Ivan a few useful words while the two of you are waiting?'

I picked up a pencil and one of the very few cards that hadn't yet got somebody's name written at the top. 'She wants me to teach you one or two useful words while we're waiting.'

'Fine,' Ivan said. 'I'll choose the words. You write them down in English. Start, please, with: "He is a mean-spirited turnip".'

He had said please! I felt quite proud that my good manners were at last brushing off on him. I didn't want to introduce a sour note, so I sat down and wrote 'He is a mean-spirited turnip' neatly on one of the spare cards.

'Right!' Ivan said. 'Now please do: "She is as crazy as a rat in a bag".'

He had said please again. So I wrote that out too.

'Next!' he said. 'Please do: "Oh, she may well have a merry smile on her lips but, believe me, she has evil in her heart".'

'That's not going to be frightfully useful,' I warned him.

'As useful as the others.'

And since there was no arguing with that, I wrote down that one as well. Then, finally, Mrs Blaizely finished her phone call.

'Ivan,' she said. 'You can stay over there at the table for the moment. Right now I only need Boris.'

She beckoned me closer. 'Boris, could you translate this for me, please?'

She handed over one of Ivan's sheets from the assessment.

'But this is maths,' I said. 'And it's far too hard for me to explain. I'm still struggling with simple fractions.'

'No, Boris,' said Mrs Blaizely patiently. 'Look on the back.'

I turned it over and realised that, when I slid off to the lavatory thinking that Ivan was doing fine by himself with the maths, he'd flipped the page and written (in Russian):

I <u>beg</u> you to help me. I have been kidnapped. That woman who dragged me into St Edmund's this morning is not my mother. She stole me from the orphanage, smuggled me over the border, and now she plans to –'

There it stopped.

'Well?' Mrs Blaizely prompted. 'What does it say? Miss Honeyman thought that it might be a request for extra time, or perhaps a short note from Ivan to explain why he doesn't show his working.'

'He doesn't show his working because he finds the sums so easy he does them in his head,' I said.

'Is that what this note says?'

'No,' I admitted. I thought of telling her what it did say. But then I had a far, far better idea: a really civilized way of putting an end to a wrong-headed favour and a horrible duty.

So I told Mrs Blaizely, 'What it says is: "I think it might have been a big mistake to

81

make me go round with Boris. Charming and helpful as he has been, I'd pick up English much faster without an interpreter at my side."'

'How thoughtful!' said Mrs Blaizely. 'You see, he didn't want to hurt your feelings by making you say that while he was standing beside you.'

I didn't have anything either good-mannered or positive to say, so I didn't say anything. I just stood there scuffing my feet on her carpet.

Mrs Blaizely was gazing at Ivan fondly across the room. 'He's clearly going to fit in here at St Edmund's very well indeed. He's obviously sensitive. And he hates saying anything in the slightest bit nasty.'

I coughed politely. It was the best that I could do.

Mrs Blaizely added admiringly, 'Look at him, sitting there copying out the words you've just shown him so busily. Not wasting any time. He is a lovely, lovely boy and we are lucky to have him.'

I couldn't help it. It isn't positive. It isn't good-mannered. It isn't even civilized.

But I still said it.

'*Vu navernoye ne znayete chto vse detee storonaytsa vashego lubimchicka Vanu, e dazhe sobaki obhodyat ego storonoy esli on ne veshaet kuski svininu okrug sheiye.*'

Mrs Blaizely stared at me. 'What was that, Boris? Say it in English, please.'

I told her blandly, 'What I just said was, "Yes, it's been nothing but a pleasure to walk around with him today. He's been cooperative and appreciative, and I expect that we'll soon be firm friends."'

Good thing she doesn't speak Russian. Or she'd have known right from the start that what I really said was:

'That Ivan you're getting so fond of is

actually a troublesome little white goblin who'd have to hang a pork chop round his neck to get the dogs to play with him.'

That's how fed up I was.

9

In which rescue arrives in the shape of a very angry mother, great musical talent, and a small mistake

Back in the classroom, Miss Honeyman set us designing 'My Perfect City'. I started with an outdoor swimming pool while Ivan began with an abattoir. I put in a few parks as Ivan chose where to put his string of gambling casinos. I planned a huge hospital as he decided on the right place for his Waste Incineration plant. I was just thinking about my riverside cycling paths when Mrs Blaizely tapped on the classroom door.

'I've finally got to the end of all Ivan's assessment sheets,' she told Miss Honeyman. 'Can I borrow him – and Boris as well, of course – so I can discuss the

results with him?'

'We have to go with her,' I told Ivan.

Ivan reached under the desk for his red leather-bound oboe case, making it clear he was quite sure he'd be moved up a class, and couldn't be bothered to come back long enough to fetch his oboe and to say goodbye.

Then he stood up. As soon as he reached the door he turned to give Miss Honeyman one of his smart little bows from the waist. 'Stay with your flock of mindless chickens,' he told her. 'Keep up your Work with the Witless. I have better things to do and finer places to be.'

He beamed, and she beamed back and asked me, 'What did he say?'

I was so angry with Ivan, I very nearly managed to tell her. But I am fond of Miss Honeyman. And she'd have been so upset. So I just told her, 'He says it's been a pleasure doing the work with you. And though it's very nearly the end of the afternoon, he hopes he'll be back in time to finish his Perfect City.'

'That's nice,' she said. 'I only wish that everyone in St Edmund's could be as charming.'

We set off down the corridor, with Mrs Blaizely beaming as well. You could tell she, too, was hoping Ivan's manners were catching. I was so furious I nearly blurted out the truth, 'You and Miss Honeyman would be making a jumbo-sized mistake if you want the rest of us to get more like him. That would be curtains for your civilized school.'

I bit my tongue, though. And just at that moment we reached the turn in the corridor, and Ivan took the chance to smirk.

And that was when I lost it. Yes, *me*. I simply couldn't stand it any more. I'd had enough of watching him spend the day making fools of all of us and an especially big fool of me.

I scoured my brain for the worst insult I could find. The trouble is that we're such a civilized school that I was out of practice. So by the time I'd realised that I couldn't think of anything, we were in Mrs Blaizely's room and it was too late anyway.

She sat at the desk and picked up Ivan's assessment papers.

'Right,' she said, running her fingers down the columns on his score card. 'The first thing to tell him is that he's obviously very, very bright indeed.'

I took revenge. 'She says you're too clever by half,' I snapped at Ivan.

'And has a most enquiring mind.'

'She says you're nosy.'

'He's clearly tremendously artistic.'

'You're probably clingy and

oversensitive and a bit of a mummy's boy.'

'And he is obviously particularly musical.'

'And you're a giant great show-off with your big loud voice.'

'He's self-motivated.' She paused and gave me a worried look. 'That means –'

'I know what it means,' I told her, and turned to Boris. 'She says you're good at working by yourself, probably because the teachers avoid you and you have no friends.'

'He's imaginative.'

'You're a shocking liar.'

'Confident.'

'Bossy.'

'Cheerful by nature.'

'Too stupid to worry about things.'

'And very independent.'

'Probably a criminal.'

'He's –'

She broke off because of a fearful rattling at the door. All of us turned to stare.

In burst an angry woman. It was Ivan's mother. I recognised her from the scene at the school gates that morning.

'Ivan! Ivan! What are you *doing* here?' she shrieked in Russian.

Ivan said sourly, 'What do you think? I'm doing exactly what you told me.'

'Bah!' Out of the angry woman's mouth poured a torrent of Russian, some of

it quite rude, mostly about what a stupid school her son was standing in, and how a whole day had been wasted. She was so furious that Mrs Blaizely stood up and hurried around the desk to stand in front of Ivan and me to protect us. Ivan kept poking his head out to the side and trying to stem his mother's flow of fury by reminding her, 'I did keep *warning* you. I kept on pointing to the sign and telling you, "That does not say Welcome to St Edward's, it says St Edmund's".'

Suspicion stirred in my mind. One of the things about Russian is that the letters look quite different. So if you're going to learn the language, you have to start with a whole new alphabet.

And that works both ways . . .

Ivan was still arguing back. 'I *kept* on telling you. But would you listen? No. You just dragged me in here, and dumped me at

the school office. So the whole wasted day is all your fault.'

St Edmund's . . . St Edward's . . .

If you hadn't learned the English alphabet – and really quite well – you might not notice the difference.

Ivan's mother was practically screeching at him now. '*My* fault? I pay for you to come halfway across the world for better lessons and this is how you behave!'

For better lessons? Well, not in maths, that was for sure. Ivan was streets ahead of all of us. And not in singing, either. He was as good as anyone else in the class. And his writing was pretty fluent and colourful, whichever way you translated it.

Now Ivan was leaning around Mrs Blaizely to shout back at his mother. 'It's not my fault Professor Borotsky decided to move halfway across the world to Stupid Town!'

Mrs Blaizely leaned down and whispered in my ear, 'Boris, have you the slightest idea what they are quarrelling about?'

You didn't have to be Sherlock Holmes to work out what had happened. 'It's perfectly simple,' I told her. 'Ivan's oboe teacher is called Professor Borotsky. Right now he must be teaching up the road at St Edward's Music School. Ivan was supposed to go there to carry on studying with him, and ended up in our school by mistake because his mother didn't read the sign right and wouldn't listen when Ivan tried to correct her.'

Ivan turned my way. 'Well done, Little Beanbrain,' he muttered (in Russian) behind Mrs Blaizely's back.

'I *knew* you understood English all the time,' I whispered back to him. 'I was just playing along with you to pass the time.'

'Oh no, you weren't, Squirrelbrain!'

'Yes, I was, Nosebleed!'

'Are you two quarrelling as well now?' Mrs Blaizely asked.

'No,' I said firmly. 'He's simply thanking me warmly for being such an enormous help to him and he asked me to tell you he's very, very sorry that he's got to leave our school now and he won't be back.' I took a deep breath. '*Ever.*'

Mrs Blaizely shook her head. 'Oh, dear.' Her disappointment was obvious. 'But I suppose it's all for the best.'

'Yes,' I said. '*I* think it is.'

'If he's so *very* talented . . .'

'If!'

'Watch it,' warned Ivan. He seemed about to unclasp his oboe case and show us just how talented he was. But clearly his mother reckoned her son had wasted more than enough time already in stupid St Edmund's, and ought to be getting up the street to see Professor Borotsky.

'Please tell him,' said Mrs Blaizely, 'that I hope he has a really good time at his new music school. And tell him not to feel too bad about leaving his very good friend –'

'His very good friend?'

'*You*,' she explained. 'Because, frankly, it was quite obvious from his assessment that he couldn't stay in your class. He was far too far ahead to waste a whole year going over stuff he already knew.'

I regretted not being able to tell him, 'She says you'd have been put down into the nursery anyhow.' But now that I knew he understood English perfectly, there was no point. And anyway, with his mother standing there listening, I would never have dared.

'Well, goodbye then,' I said. I gave Boris one of his own smart little bows from the waist, and stuck out my hand.

He shook it.

'Bye, mate!' he said (in Russian).

At the door, he turned. 'Oh, by the way,' he added, 'I left you a little present.'

'Where?'

He pointed to the cards stacked on the table and he winked.

Then, with one last bow, he was gone.

10

In which a lot of parents come up to the school to complain about report cards

I went back to the classroom. There were only a few minutes left before the last bell, and I wanted to add a bit more to my Perfect City. I put in a children's play park and an ice-skating rink and a funfair and a duckpond. But my heart wasn't in it because I was really still thinking about Ivan.

At first I was telling myself it was a good thing he hadn't stayed at our school. He hadn't fitted in. He wasn't polite. He didn't have a positive attitude. And he certainly wasn't civilized.

So it was lucky he was so good at music and had gone off to St Edward's before anyone except me realised what he was like.

And then another thought struck. I loved our singing classes. (Look how frustrated I'd felt when I'd been dragged out of one.) But even I didn't love singing so much that I would let myself be uprooted from my school to travel halfway across the world to get more lessons from a favourite teacher.

Ivan loved his oboe that much. And then a whole day had been totally wasted.

I'd have been fed up, too. I'd have been so frustrated that, instead of trying to explain and get my mother back to take me further up the street to the right school, I might have gone into a giant sulk and spent the day pretending I couldn't understand a word of English – not even 'Hi!' – and saying the worst things I could think of to everyone round me.

I was still thinking when Miss Honeyman called out, 'Time's up,' and ambled round the classroom, collecting our work sheets. When she reached Ivan's desk, she picked up his paper and said regretfully, 'No point in keeping this if he's not coming back.'

She dropped it in the huge waste paper bin. I watched it floating down on top of all the sweet wrappers and crumpled notes and torn-up bits of paper, and thought I'd like to keep it as a souvenir of my strange day with Ivan.

So, as I was walking past after the last bell rang, I picked it out.

Since I'd last glanced at it, Ivan had added a few more things to his Perfect City: a scrap yard, a crematorium and a home for lost dogs. (He certainly was a fast worker.)

As I began to fold it, I noticed

something written on the back. I turned it over to see he'd written (in Russian *and* in English): 'Bye then, Boris. You were a real pal. Thanks for everything.'

*

That wasn't the only thing Ivan left behind him. I had a good laugh the day after our class took home their report cards. As Mrs Blaizely said, Ivan had certainly kept himself busy when he had his back to us, writing at that table. Oriole's mother was outraged to read in Oriole's report card that her daughter was as crazy as a rat in a bag.

Yusef's parents were none too delighted to learn that their son was a mean-spirited turnip.

And Lulu's parents were very startled indeed to learn that, though a merry smile plays around her lips, their daughter had evil in her heart.

Me? Well, I just notice every single oboe I hear, and smile to myself as I remember Ivan.

Oh, yes. And I can't listen to the infants

singing any of their sweet little nursery rhymes without a chill running down my spine . . .

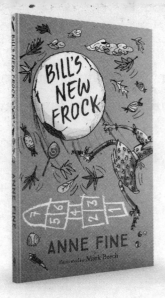

'Anne Fine is an author who knows how to make readers laugh'
The Guardian

Read all of Anne Fine's hilarious stories of classroom chaos